First published in Great Britain in 2018 by Cornish Book Company

A Hilliard Publishing Company
Wadebridge, Cornwall

Illustrations by Paul Winward
Book design by Neil Coe

A catalogue record for this book is available from the British Library

ISBN 978-0-9935352-3-9

Cornish Book Company
www.cornishbookcompany.com

CORNISH BOOK COMPANY

For the real Captain Seasick!

Can you find Benny the Blenny, the fish who is afraid of the sea, hiding in every picture?

You will need to look very carefully!

## THE TOMPOT BLENNY

### FACT BOX

**1.** The Tompot Blenny is a small, mottled brown, inquisitive fish, with a smooth slimy body. Its eyes are high up on its head, along with two small antlers. It has a long fin with an orange edge and a blue dot on it, which runs the length of its body. In mating season, the male Tompot Blenny changes colour to attract a mate, it then stays with any eggs, guarding them until they hatch.

**2.** The Tompot Blenny hides in cracks and crevices in the rocks or under seaweed. It does not need to be in the water, but it must always be somewhere damp.

**3.** The Tompot Blenny eats small prawns, ragworm, lugworm and other small invertebrates.

SPLAAAT! SPLAAAT! SPLAAAT!

Seagull poo dripped down Captain Seasick's shoulder.

"Jumping jellyfish and bubbling barnacles!" exclaimed Captain Seasick as he wiped it away with a big spotted handkerchief. "That means good luck! No doubt about it!"

"I'll be having a good catch today, me 'ansome," Captain Seasick called to old Half Pint, who was barely bigger than a Cornish pisky, and the landlord of The Itchy Crab Inn. "Just been bombed by a seagull, and you know what that means!"

"Arrrrrr," answered Half Pint. "I'll be putting fish supper on the menu tonight then – bring it straight into the kitchen when you get back to shore."

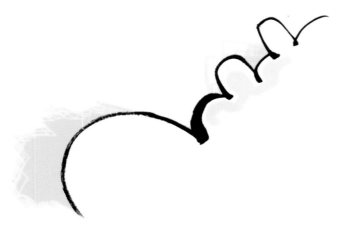

But something wasn't quite right. As Captain Seasick clambered aboard *Up She Comes*, he had an uncomfortable feeling that he was being watched. Sure enough, on the very top of the flagpole of his rainbow-striped boat, above the black and white flag of St. Piran, sat a fat, slightly mean-looking seagull, its beady yellow eyes fixed intently on Captain Seasick, watching his every move. Captain Seasick tried to ignore the bird, started the engine, and began to slowly steer *Up She Comes* out of the estuary, towards the open sea.

The fat seagull didn't move.

Out along the estuary *Up She Comes* quietly chugged: past the big crane in the boat yard; past the Harbour Master's office; past Splosh the ferryman with his boat full of tourists and his scruffy dog Salty; past the row of pretty, white fishermen's cottages; and past The Itchy Crab Inn with its colourful bunting flying.

And still the little boat motored on, past The Block House where a chain used to cross the estuary to stop pirate ships from entering the harbour and past the funny lady's big house next to Windy Bottom Beach.

UP SHE COMES

Still the fat seagull sat atop the flagpole of Captain Seasick's stripy boat, its yellow eyes never blinking, watching Captain Seasick very carefully.

Captain Seasick stopped his engine. "Time for a spot of brunch to settle my belly before I start fishing," he said, glancing cautiously at the mean seagull.

The seagull sat and stared as Captain Seasick tucked into his favourite steak and Cornish Blue pasty. It made Captain Seasick feel just a tiny bit uncomfortable. "Don't be silly! It's just a seagull," he told himself.

"NASTY PASTY! NASTY PASTY!"

the seagull seemed to screech loudly.

"Tastes good to me," mumbled Captain Seasick, his mouth full of crumbly pasty. "Now, just room for one or two of those delicious cupcakes I got from The Seagull's Lunchbox Bakery this morning, before I get fishing."

Captain Seasick opened his mouth wide to take a huge bite of his favourite sweet treat at the exact same moment that the fat seagull swooped towards him and snatched the sticky peanut butter goodie right out of his huge, shovel-sized hand.

**"Dithering dolphins!"** exclaimed Captain Seasick to the seagull. "If that was what you wanted you should have said! I'd have been happy to share!"

But the seagull didn't look happy. In fact, as it guzzled down Captain Seasick's lovely, gooey cake, it looked meaner and angrier than ever.

WALLOP! SPLAAAT!

SPLAAAT! WALLOP!

The seagull dive-bombed Captain Seasick, swooping fast and low towards him, dropping poop bombs all over the deck of *Up She Comes*.

"Fluttering flat fish!" stammered a flabbergasted Captain Seasick. "There's no need for that you know!" (And there'll be no more cake sharing after that performance either, he thought to himself.) "Now, time I caught some fish." And with that, Captain Seasick cast his rod long and hard, out into the open sea.

The fat, angry seagull landed heavily on the roof of the little boat's cabin, stared evilly at Captain Seasick and began to squawk and rain dance at the same time, stamping its feet up and down, and nodding its head madly.

Captain Seasick tried to ignore the grumpy bird, and hummed a little hum to himself:

Fishy, fishy in the sea,

Fishy, fishy come to me...

The seagull squawked louder and stamped harder and faster, its head bobbing up and down, up and down, up and down.

Captain Seasick hummed louder and concentrated hard on the tip of his rod.

Fishy, fishy in the sea,

Come to me, I want my tea!

"SQUAWK! SQUAWK!" cried the angry seagull, with attitude.

Right at that moment, Captain Seasick felt a familiar churning in his belly. His face turned a spooky shade of green and sweat dripped from his nose. His legs began to tremble inside his yellow waders, his head started to spin, and his belly began to gurgle loudly.

"SQUAWK!" screeched the angry seagull again, still madly performing its rain dance on the cabin roof.

PAAAAAAARP! went Captain Seasick, as a huge rasping thunder crack of a trump blasted from one end.

"TRUMPET TROUSERS! STINKY BUM!" screeched the angry seagull, turning its bobbing head away, but still stamping its feet.

BURRRRP! went Captain Seasick, as a loud smelly belch of wind escaped from the other.

"STAND CLEAR!" screamed the angry seagull.

Wobbling winkles! Captain Seasick was about to explode!

That lovely pasty (which Mrs. Seasick had baked fresh that morning) was trying to break free, to escape from Captain Seasick's belly one way or another.

"SQUAWK!" went the mean gull.

SWOOOOSH! went Captain Seasick's brunch.

Up it came, splashing into the clear blue sea below and turning the gentle waves into a swirling mess of pasty, cupcakes...carrots and sweetcorn!

Carrots and sweetcorn? Where had they come from? Captain Seasick hadn't eaten either of those today!

"POTTY MOUTH! NAPPY BREATH!" screeched the angry seagull, swooping around Captain Seasick's head.

Lots more seagulls had gathered to watch and laugh as Captain Seasick hurled the contents of his belly over the rainbow-striped side of *Up She Comes*, and into the now colourful sea.

"NAPPY BREATH! POTTY MOUTH!" they all squawked together.

"Munting mackerel!" mumbled poor Captain Seasick as another loud, stinky, repeating popcorn trump blasted from his bottom, and the onlooking seagulls turned their heads away in disgust.

POP, POP, POP, POP, POP, PAAAAARP!

"Perhaps I shouldn't have eaten that last cupcake?" Captain Seasick thought aloud. "But blistering barnacles! Where did those carrots and sweetcorn come from?"

"POTTY MOUTH! NAPPY BREATH!" screeched the laughing seagulls over and over again as they dive-bombed Captain Seasick and the swirling sea of pasty and cupcakes.

But the angry seagull – the mean gull – stood perfectly still, eyeing up Captain Seasick with a steely, yellow stare.

# "Jumping jelly fish!"

exclaimed Captain Seasick. At that very moment, while he was still catching his breath, there was a huge tug on his fishing line.

Grabbing the rod and trying to polish his little round glasses at the same time, Captain Seasick's twinkly, piercing, but extremely short-sighted blue eyes peered towards the end of his line. And so too did the angry seagull.

What Captain Seasick saw looked like a very small polar bear, and it was now moving steadily towards his boat as he wound his reel in.

"Plopping penguins!" exclaimed Captain Seasick. "Surely there can't be polar bears in Cornish waters?"

"BLIND AS A BAT! BLIND AS A BAT!" laughed the circling seagulls.

As the end of his line got closer, Captain Seasick could feel a strange shivering. Whatever he had caught was certainly shaking quite furiously. Even the angry seagull had fallen silent now, and was staring intently out to sea, standing perfectly still, back on its perch at the top of the flag pole.

Captain Seasick carefully leaned over the side of *Up She Comes*, and reached cautiously into the sea below. Gently, he lifted out his catch and laid it on the wooden deck.

A pair of scared, blinking, yellow eyes looked out from a white plastic prison. Slowly, so as not to alarm whatever was in there, Captain Seasick reached into the tattered plastic to discover a fluffy, brown, and extremely bedraggled baby seagull, entangled in an old supermarket carrier bag.

The angry seagull was not dancing and squawking now. And the circling seagulls had all swooped down to the sea where they were gently bobbing up and down. All beady yellow eyes were watching Captain Seasick and his catch of the day.

Slowly and calmly, Captain Seasick took off his woolly beany hat, setting his wild, curly hair free, and gently placed the shivering baby seagull inside it. He turned the engine on and began to steer *Up She Comes* back to the quay. 'Enough excitement for one day,' thought Captain Seasick. 'And no fish suppers for The Itchy Crab diners tonight!'

As Captain Seasick secured *Up She Comes* to her mooring, the angry seagull, who was definitely much happier now, swooped down to claim her baby.

"HAPPY DAYS! HAPPY DAYS!" she squawked quietly.

Captain Seasick suddenly realised the angry seagull hadn't been angry at all. The angry seagull had just wanted Captain Seasick to help rescue her baby!

Later that evening, Captain Seasick sat at home in his comfy chair, with a glass of his favourite Cornish scrumpy in his hand, looking out of the window of "Puffin Top", his little house on the hill. He watched the sea beyond and the seagulls flying home to roost with their young.

"Jumping jelly fish!" Captain Seasick thought proudly to himself. "I've been a seagull superhero today! No fish for tea, mind, but that was a PROPER JOB!"

# MORE IN THE CAPTAIN SEASICK SERIES

COMING SOON

### Captain Seasick
### and the Giant Pasty

### Captain Seasick's
### Military Operation

### Captain Seasick's
### Royal Appointment

### Captain Seasick's
### Shark Alert